SHIKARAS IN THE RAIN

Based on Nila's lost and found diary - Kashmir Days

A NOVELLA BASED ON TRUE INCIDENTS

CYRIL MUKALEL

POTTER'S WHEEL PUBLISHING HOUSE MINNEAPOLIS

SHIKARAS IN THE RAIN by CYRIL MUKALEL

Published by POTTER'S WHEEL PUBLISHING HOUSE MINNEAPOLIS MN 55378

www.POTTERSWHEELPUBLISHING.com

For permissions contact: info@POTTERSWHEELPUBLISHING.com

Foreword

I was destined to read that diary; it was my destiny to know Nila and her world as I travel through her scribbles in that diary. The few pages in that journal expand into the book where the reader becomes a participant in the journey that begins in Kashmir and explores other parts of the world.

What would happen if you chance upon a mysterious journal? Perhaps your curiosity will compel you to open it and read *just* the first few lines. Just then, at that precise moment, those lines cause something to happen in your life- something fated to happen.

Go for a short journey through the pages of Nila's diary as she tells about Saraswati's epic ordeal. You may also discover that life itself, is a mysterious phenomenon. You will see the past, the present, and the future as they chase each other in a circle set in motion by destiny. You will see that sometimes the future becomes the present in a premonitory dream- in a prophecy. You will realize that we know so little about life, yet we love to lock ourselves in cages of judgment.

Sometimes we live in someone's mind

A stolen heart beating

Like the ageless sages left their bodies naked

Their minds trapped in the Himalayan mist

We see the dreams belong to someone

Unleashing it on a kite

Trusting the line we never control

Blotted ink stain covering the obituary column

Hiding everything under

Shikaras In The Rain

When the cuckoo broke the long silence to coo eight times, Nila was already awake. She ignored it and continued to flirt with the sunlight intruding into her bedroom through the slits of the red velvet window drapes. As she tilted her golden anklets, she reflected the light to make tiny star- dust around Lord Krishna's picture hung on the wall. The clock was her companion in seclusion, and a major reason for the little tension that fumed between them in the initial days she moved to the US. The sound of the cuckoo gave her a false feeling that she was close to her home, and all her dear ones were within walking distance away.

"No human can survive you, Chatterbox, not even this mechanical bird." That was how Ashok made fun of her when she argued to have the cuckoo clock go off every fifteen minutes, like the Grandfather clock in her parent's home. Ashok reasoned this bizarre behavior to be part of Nila's loneliness, and the creative mind she claimed to have.

He always hesitated to satisfy Nila's demands as he could never understand her reasoning, but later he always succumbed to avoid ruining the serenity.

For Nila, when her husband was at work, the clock gave her comfort and curbed her loneliness. It was a companion who patiently listened to her crazy thoughts and nodded at regular intervals. Cuckoo was the most ideal friend she could ever ask for, as it had all the qualities to get along with an extrovert like her. It had the patience to listen to all her whims and all her never-ending stories. The cuckoo clock was a wedding gift from Auntie Molly, someone who was very dear to her, the one who took care of her and was there for her as her own mother from the day she was born.

When Ashok's marriage proposal came for their arranged marriage, everyone in the family thought he was the perfect match for Nila. He was well-educated and exceptionally well-mannered, but there was a fear in everyone to send her off in marriage to a faraway place like America, with very different customs. It was Auntie Molly who convinced everyone and stood as the guarantor for the wedding. Auntie and her husband Alex lived in a place close to Ashok's city, which gave everyone confidence. In case something needed to be looked into, Auntie was only a few hours away.

It was a long-awaited day for Nila... a trip to Auntie's home. This was something she had wanted to do in the first month of her arrival in the US, but it had taken almost a year to happen. It had been postponed a few times with Ashok's work commitments. This time she had left everything to God, and prayed fervently to Lord Ganesh, the ultimate power, to confiscate any obstacles, to avoid any last-minute delays in their travel plans. She had picked the dress to wear the day before and baked a fruitcake a few days earlier. She planned a surprise for Auntie by making a collage with pictures from her collection she began gathering from her primary school days and onward.

"Wake up, Ashok, let's get ready quickly, and start at nine as we planned last night."

Nila shook her husband to wake him.

"Come on, you are not even letting me sleep late on a long weekend? There is nothing much to get ready for. A quick shower and I will be on the road. It's you who needs two hours to put makeup on and delays everything," he continued in a mocking voice. "You know the later we go the less we need to listen to the so-called Uncle Alex's fake stories of bravery. Even a cook retired from the military would claim to have shot down a helicopter." He chuckled.

"Shut up, Ashok; you should respect people who risked their lives for their country. He is a gentleman. And you know what? He is a very successful businessman owning several gas stations in the city. I hope he is home and not busy when we get there."

"I bet he will be there, especially when he has admirers like you wanting to listen to him." Ashok sounded like a whining kid, jealous over losing importance in the eyes of his wife.

Nila continued in a broken voice, "Ashok; you don't know how dear they are to me. You will realize how nice they are one day; they are probably far better than anyone you have ever met."

"Oh... let us not go further on that," Ashok replied, confining her. Nila jumped out of the bed to show her frustration and went to the living room, where she always found something to calm herself down with.

She looked through the pictures on the collage she had made as a gift for Auntie. She began to cheer a little while looking at a faded picture that was taken with a Polaroid camera. The picture was sent to her after Auntie Molly had reached the US for the first time. She looked thin and pale, but beautiful, with the Statue of Liberty in the backdrop.

Auntie had written behind the picture that she had to be in New York for a month, to attend training before she could begin to work. Glancing through the pictures from her childhood made Nila nostalgic and brought memories to dampen her eyes.

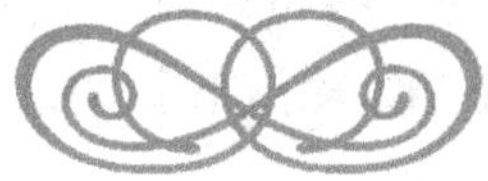

Although Auntie Molly was not her mother's younger sister or even related to her in any way, Nila used to call her *Chitta*. But all the kids in the neighborhood began to address her as 'Auntie' after she came to the village to visit for the first time since leaving for the US. They felt that treating her like a local woman may not be appropriate, and they found delight in calling her "American Auntie." A big crowd of relatives and neighbors had gathered in their home to celebrate her arrival. Kids were playing in the back-yard and around the haystack waiting for Auntie to arrive from the airport, which was a three-hour car journey. When the wind bustled, or the water wheel in the rice field swayed with a sudden gush, kids ran into the dirt road screaming, "She is here!" and waited until the sound faded away. They all waited, hoping to eat a stomach full of chocolates and candies when she opened her luggage. After a long wait, when *Chitta* got out of the black ambassador car, almost everyone wowed and had their eyebrows arched in astonishment.

The change from a naïve village girl into a sophisticated *American Madam* was not something the poor villagers could digest easily. Everyone looked in disbelief at the one who had left clad in a saree to return in jeans and top. Her long hair was cut by half and curled at the tip. With her threaded eyebrows and glossy lips, she looked like a celebrity on the cover page of *Vanitha* Malayalam women's magazine. Kids hesitated to go near her until a naughty kid screamed, "Our *American-Madaamma* is finally here." Everyone laughed in amusement. Nila didn't go near her at first because she felt a distance she'd never had before. But the kids who went near her said she had a beautiful smell that was sweeter than the Arabian perfume worn by people returning from Dubai.

In those days, Auntie was the topic of conversation in the local tea stalls and corner shops where people gathered to gossip and smoke locally made *beedi*. Some pranksters even spread the rumor that she was there to look for a new husband after she got tired of her American husband.

Auntie Molly's family had been their neighbor way before Nila was born. But, they were more than just neighbors; they were part of the family, always around, tending to and spending time in their home. Molly was the oldest and sweetest amongst the four girls. Amma once told her how they came to the village. They were part of a group of *Syrian Christian* families who migrated from Kottayam in the Travancore region. Those hardworking families turned the barren, rocky land, inhabited by poisonous snakes, into plantations. Her father, Mathaichan, was a sincere and honest man. When communism was spreading in the area, he helped Nila's father settle the labor dispute and protect the family from an ambush common against landlords at that time. People in the village respected him, and due to the booming tourism industry, they even named the northern hill in his name as Mathai Mala. It's now been renamed to Mathew Hills. Mathaichan toiled to turn that rocky hill into green, filling it with tapioca plants, a remnant from the Portuguese invasion a few centuries ago. *Kappa* produced from the plants later became the staple food for the poor in the whole region. Later, he was the one who introduced rubber trees to the region, which made most peasants rich.

Mathaichan used to work from early morning till sundown, cultivating yucca known as *Kappa* locally, and rubber trees on the hill, and rice in the rice field. On Friday evenings, he walked to the other side of the hill to drink *Arrack,* homemade liquor made by distilling toddy from the coconut palm. On his way home, he bought sizzling *Parippu-vada,* lentil discs fried in coconut oil, from the teashop. All the kids waited for the treat. Drunk and zigzagging back home, he made sure the *Parippu-vada* was still fresh. He kept them warm covered in layers of newspaper under his armpit. He turned his armpit into a walking oven! They all sat on the half wall of portico eating Parippu-vada, then got a stomach full of skinned *kappa,* boiled and cooked along with fresh hot pepper sauce. Nila's mom fried sardines dipped in spicy sauce to go along with the *Kappa.* Once tired of eating, they all went down to the courtyard and sat around a kerosene lamp. Then Mathaichan would sing folk songs from Kottayam, and teach them *Margam Kali,* a traditional dance played to songs narrating the stories based on the evangelization by St. Thomas, the Apostle, in India.

Friday nights gave everyone vivid memories that none of them would ever forget. But like an untimely monsoon that blazed through the sky and drowned everything below, strings of tragedies charred all their dreams in its fury.

On a sunny, humid morning, while Mathaichan was clearing the weeds among tapioca plant bushes, a saw-scaled viper blended among the dry leaves pressed its fangs into his left lower calf, filling it with venom. He quickly turned around and chopped the snake into two halves before he collapsed. It was only after an hour that his wife, Susanna, found him while bringing him breakfast. He was unconscious with froth all over his mouth. She screamed for help, and he was taken to the village *vishahari*, the local poison specialist, but he couldn't do much. His foot had turned black by then and later at the government hospital, doctors amputated the dead foot from below his knee. The venom that took the foot of the breadwinner also cast a dark shadow over the life of four girls and their helpless mother. As a healthy man, he never sat idle or fell sick in his entire life. He was struggling to handle his new situation. Later, his courage and physical strength drained. It didn't get any better. Following monsoon hit his fields sending a gushing mudslide that took out all the hard work he had put in for decades. That was too much for him to handle. His health deteriorated quickly, his frail mind and ailing body couldn't survive that rainy season.

Nila's family was there for his family, but it was hard to go through. When Molly decided to go to America, the family finally emerged from the years-long haze and pain. Their story was a living lesson for Nila and everyone who knew them. Nila always found strength, as it didn't matter how weak one was or the graveness of troubles one went through, what really mattered was finding a way to keep the mind strong and fearlessly fighting the fight to overcome one's own fears. The family struggled to survive. To make their living, Molly quit going to school and helped her mom doing menial chores for many affluent families. After a few years of struggle, and seeing no way to bounce back to normalcy, Molly joined a convent to become a nun. There she completed high school and studied nursing to serve the poor in the remote villages of northern India. During that time, Nila was a schoolgirl and Auntie used to visit her home once every year. She always stopped at Nila's home to see her first, as there was an inherent bond between them. She was there always when Nila grew up, and she was like her own child. Amma used to tell Nila that when she was little she used to cry hysterically for hours until Auntie held her.

On every visit, Auntie gifted Nila with oversized woolen sweaters donated to the monastery by people living in western countries. After she completed her studies, a missionary priest who knew about her family's dismal state asked Auntie to leave the order to help her family and arranged for her to go to America.

Nila recalled the day Auntie left for America. Everyone followed the slow-moving white ambassador car, biding Molly goodbye along the way until it reached the train station. Keeping all her emotions to herself, Molly smiled and waved while standing at the train door. Everyone watched her as the train disappeared over those parallel lines that merged in the distance. They all wept, as they all loved her and knew they may not see her for a very long time. But the mood transformed into a happy one when they all turned to see her mother smiling, which hardly anyone had seen in a long time. She had learned that tears were worth more when shed in joy.

Nila wiped her teary eyes with the back of her hand, and continued staring at the old pictures in the living room.

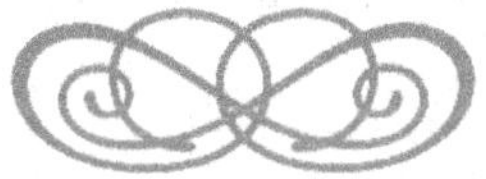

It was past noon by the time they reached Auntie Molly's home. Stepping out of the car into the driveway, they got a taste of the warmth that was waiting for them. The over-worked kitchen exhaust fan continued to swirl the smell of freshly fried beef cutlets and curried fish into the entire neighborhood. Unable to hold their excitement,

Auntie and Uncle came running outside to receive them. Stroking Nila's arm, Auntie said with affection, "We were worried... Did you get lost on the way?"

"Oh, no, we started a little late. There was construction on the way," Nila said with an ecstatic smile.

Except for the thick mustache with tips pointed up like the old Air India mascot, Uncle looked nothing like a typical retired Indian military person. He had long curly hair which hung loosely just above the shoulders, hanging out of his baseball cap. The cap was there to cover his shiny bald head which was evident by the smooth forehead and thin sideburns His small round pot-belly complemented his happy face and puffy cheeks. Shallow eyes showed he was as sincere as he looked. The smile on his face and the attention he gave them spilled over with love and affection in his heart. Ashok instantly fell for Uncle's simplicity, and his reluctance at coming disappeared instantly.

"Come, children, come. Let's go in." Uncle in his affectionate voice persuaded them.

"Wow!" Nila was amazed by the gorgeous home and scanned the inside while removing her sandals. The Cathedral Ceiling with a gigantic French chandelier and the large bay windows in the living room gave the home a Grande look. After sitting on the hand-carved Chinese sofa, Ashok peaked out of the window that overlooked a large pond with a private walking trail around it. Two snow-white swans were idly floating by. As they looked at each other, they made a squished heart symbol with their long necks.

From the kitchen, Nila walked toward the family room, browsing the Italian themed-cabinets built around the fireplace in dark cherry wood. Its contents displayed a snapshot of their artistic taste. Ashok joined Nila in looking at the miniature houseboats with elephants carved in the teak wood. Chess pieces in crystal were arranged without the board. The pawns had been chiseled to look like human faces which Ashok thought had probably been picked by their children. A shelf at the top was filled with trophies and medals their kids had won during their school days. Above the TV were spotlights that sparkled on their magnificent stone collection. Some of them had silver and gold sparkling.

Auntie opened the glass door and took out a small shiny stone. She pointed at the golden flecks stuck on it and said, "This is real gold, see? All the jewelry we have used to be like this. We got this from South Dakota when we visited

Mount Rushmore, where the presidents' faces are carved on a mountain."

Nila felt the stone and excitedly said, "Auntie, we should buy stones like this instead of too much gold jewelry. Jewelry stays in the box most of the time, but people get to enjoy it if it is something sizable and displayed like this." Everyone agreed and cheered, appreciating Nila's intended humor.

The left of the cabinet was busy with framed photographs of family members organized in different phases of their lives. The golden family tree fascinated Ashok and Nila as it held pictures of different eras and fashions. Ashok looked once again at the leaf that had Uncle's picture in it; he had no mustache and looked to be in his twenties.

"Your daughter looks exactly like you twenty years ago." Nila noticed the close resemblance of Auntie from her old picture collections.

Auntie responded with a smile. "She is in pre-med at Stanford University. Our son is doing his final year of Civil Engineering at Villanova University."

Nila nodded her head in appreciation and commented, "He is so handsome. Girls must be going crazy!"

Everyone exploded in laughter and Uncle added, "They'll both be here in the last week of August. You should definitely come over to meet them then."

While everyone chatted, Auntie had covered the large kitchen table with snacks that she had prepared. Everything was as Nila remembered from her childhood. Seeing a plateful of golden *Parippu-vada,* she was taken back to those old days, remembering Auntie's dad whose picture was in a place of pride on the family wall. "Molly, please bring some snacks downstairs, let me show Ashok the basement," Uncle said.

"Don't spoil the kid, he is not like you," Auntie said in a scolding but jovial voice and continued, "Nila, don't worry. Unless he shows his *Kottayam* style of hospitality, there won't be peace in this home until the next time you come."

Uncle smiled and gave his wife a friendly wink, "Come, Ashok, let's go downstairs." He got up from the couch and walked to the basement and Ashok followed him. Nila felt awful. She feared if Ashok were left alone with her so-called bragging uncle, she would end up paying a big price when they got back home. But she was relieved later when she heard from Ashok what had truly happened in the basement while she chatted with Auntie.

The basement looked even more fabulous than the main area of the home. Its walls had original art pieces and paintings depicting the beauty of South India. A life-sized replica of a golden caparison, which is used to cover an elephant's trunk for temple festivals, was displayed on the wall. It welcomed everyone to the basement with Kerala pride. Next to it was a large brightly colored mask depicting the expression of a *Kathakali* dancer. A world-famous handmade *Aranmula* mirror, a metallurgical wonder from Kerala, made Ashok feel like he was in an art museum. He felt the super smooth furniture with his fingers and had a quick peek at the beautiful home theater adjacent to the main hall. Ashok was amazed and he felt privileged to be in a country that had the magic of giving a retired military man from a humble beginning, and having barely finished high school, the opportunity to live such an enviable lifestyle.

Uncle turned the lights on in the other end of the basement and chortled to himself. "Come, let us sit and relax in my favorite spot in this world."

Ashok was stunned when the corner of the basement was lit up. He was overwhelmed as he approached a bar that looked more magnificent than the one in a high-end restaurant. *It would surely prompt a non-drinker to consume alcohol,* Ashok thought. He gazed at the rare collection of bottles of all shapes that had come from all around the world and was amused by a bottle with a fruit way larger than the bottle's neck. There was also a bottle, which came with gold dust in it, and a few others had dead worms in them he thought was disgusting.

"All these bottles are waiting to be tasted, which one do you want to start with?" Uncle joked to encourage him to feel free. "I am not big into drinking, Uncle. Sometimes, I have a couple of beers with friends." "Oh, my son, don't disappoint me." Uncle continued to chuckle.

Ashok responded, "Of course, I will give you company and go with whatever you suggest."

Uncle was happy with this response. It was clear from his excitement that Uncle was looking forward to having a few drinks with Ashok. He pulled a bottle from the cabinet and began to tell Ashok about his tastes and passions when it comes to drinking habits. Uncle Alex drank only Old Monk Rum, which he claimed to be his 'Regular-Use Medicine' that stood for RUM, a habit he picked up while serving the Indian military guarding the border with Pakistan. He picked up a taste for it to survive the brutal Himalayan cold, and to elude the boredom that could have eroded his sharpness.

He believed he had something in common with the Old Monk Rum; they were both first brewed in the sacred Himalayan Mountains with the souls of sages guarding over them. Those souls traveled hundreds of miles, away from their physical bodies that were still alive in the caverns hidden under the snow-covered mountains. He always felt their presence when he sipped each drop of it. His friend, who was a liquor store owner, ordered and shipped it to him from India when he ran out. Ashok watched Uncle pour the drink over the ice cubes into the crystal glasses.

Uncle raised his glass toward Ashok. "Cheers! This is not just a drink, it is a medicine. It heals the heart if you ever had a broken one, it puts your mind straight, and it will let you fight till you win." He laughed and took a long sip.

Sitting at an awkward angle, pushing on the footrest on the counter, Ashok tried to sit looking straight, and he almost lost balance and swiveled toward the left wall. His heart stopped for a moment, as he faced a wild animal. A large, stuffed buck head was hiding behind the Budweiser beer neon light on the wall. Its face was tilted down with shiny eyes looking toward him. For a moment, he thought it still had life in its eyes. Below the antlers, there was a large framed picture of beautiful Dal Lake in the midst of the Himalayan Mountains. Pointed lights made the snowcap and the houseboat roofs glow giving an extra charm to the place.

Ashok was surprised to see a real trophy buck and was curious to know how it ended up on their basement wall. Uncle told him he used to spend days in the woods on stands amid thick cover, waiting. Though he was trained to kill intruders on the border, he never had to take anyone's life but had many antlers. Auntie didn't know about his hobby for a long time. Even though she worked as a surgery nurse, she was still scared of blood and didn't like him doing it. She even threatened him saying she would run away. Uncle was not joking; Auntie had no guilt around eating steak or fried fish but couldn't digest the idea of him hunting.

Taking a quick sip out of the glass, Uncle said with pride, "It is a fourteen-pointer and my last one."

Ashok couldn't resist suppressing his curiosity. He asked why he quit hunting as he thought Auntie might have discovered his secret endeavors at some point and might have threatened to leave him.

Uncle tried to avoid answering, then he gazed at the trophy for a moment and said, "She never found out, but you know we are all brave when we are young. We dare to do anything and never think of the consequences. The moment you know you are going to become a father, you are no longer the same person... your blood no longer flows as fast as your thoughts run." Ashok sensed Uncle was not very comfortable as his voice cracked, but he didn't hinder and he continued his story.

"I watched the buck enter the cut cornfield, and I knew the stage was set; it was a three hundred pounder. The shot was taken at sixty yards and it went a bit too high. The buck went down like a rock, but soon it was on its feet and charged back into the woods. By the time I came down from the cover, it was not anywhere to be seen. There were several hoof marks where it had thrashed around before gaining its feet. I followed the blood trail marks and in ten minutes I saw him; he had fallen dead in the middle of the field. When I walked toward him, I saw a female deer next to him. Her belly fully bulged and veins netted it. I could see her tummy shaking with its fawn kicking. She stared into my eyes; I couldn't look at her again. I don't know how the deer family works, but at that moment I thought of my wife who was pregnant at the time. After that day, I couldn't hunt anymore."

By the time he finished the story, glasses were empty and Uncle refilled them quickly. Ashok was guilty of exposing the softer side of a brave soldier. He badly wanted to lighten the mood so he looked toward the beautiful scenery of Kashmir below the Antilles and began to appreciate its details.

"This ambiance of Lake Dal looks so mesmerizing with the backdrop of the snow-covered Himalayas."

Noticing Ashok's keenness in the picture, Uncle asked "Don't you love this picture? Have you ever been to Kashmir?"

Ashok shook his head.

"Oh dear, you are missing a lot... if there is heaven on Earth, that's the place." Uncle showed his passion for Kashmir and continued, "You should rent a *Shikara*, the traditional boat in the Dal Lake. Have a couple of drinks, and just stare into the Himalayas. When the sun sets, watch the sky changing colors like the passion of a Kashmiri folk dancer dancing in the moonlight till daybreak. The silver light will fade away to pour diamonds over the sky, filling it with stars you have never seen in such abundance. The oar and the waves will beat with the rhythm of your heart. The cool breeze will caress you, bringing the mystic music held in the heart of those mountains that you haven't heard. Soon you will be in a place you have never been; your mind will be one with the soul of the Himalayas and it will make you feel like you were there forever, and none of your worries had ever existed. Trust me; you will never want to leave."

He paused and turned into a philosopher. "There is something about Himalayan air. You know monks and sadhus don't feel cold. They don't feed their body; they don't age but live beyond centuries. Unlike them, we worry about the past and are anxious about the future, forgetting to live in the present. We search for peace in the midst of chaos. Like a giant bubble, we try to fill ourselves with our own ego only to see it burst into nothing, forgetting how tiny we are in this universe. Dust ... but we ..." Stifling back his feeling Uncle didn't bother to complete where he was going with his thoughts.

"Uncle, now I believe in this drink, it certainly has some magical powers. It has not only made a brave Indian soldier and a businessman out of you but a philosopher and an amazing poet, too." Ashok couldn't stop expressing his admiration. In his mind, he thought Uncle's life could be a plot for an Indian movie, except he had to handle all the archetypes and characters as he was in unison with all the archetypes, like the Tamil Movie *Dasa-avatharam*, where the actor Kamal Hasan portrayed ten characters simultaneously.

"Next time you visit your parents, you both should definitely make a trip to Kashmir." Uncle tried to persuade him.

"I'd love to go there but... it is always in the news for bad reasons, terrorism and unrest. We will... when things settle."

Uncle, with an uproarious laugh, raised his glass in one hand. Then with the other, he twirled the tip of his mustache between his thumb and forefinger. Clearing his throat, he said, "What you have heard of Militants is from the media, right?"

Ashok nodded in agreement. "I have seen them, I have walked with them, and I have fought with them," Uncle disclosed.

"Wow. That takes a lot of courage," Ashok said.

Uncle continued, "Well, we all live with some kind of fear, but the moments when we have to conquer our fears, our hearts pump faster to make our nerves stronger than steel. Our senses fall into safety mode, our lungs turn quieter, and our heartbeats in silence. Haven't you noticed your system wouldn't let you sneeze when you were in hiding and afraid of being found?"

Ashok replied, "I agree. Being part of the military must have helped you handle a lot of situations better."

"Of course it did. Anyone who got posted along the 285 kilometers on the line of control in the Jammu-Pakistan border would have a different view of life if they were lucky enough to come home alive."

Noticing Ashok's keenness to listen to his story, and being in a good mood, Uncle began to share his daring tales. He was posted at a picket, along a hostile terrain, to guard a highly dangerous and remote location in Kashmir on the India-Pakistan border. They were a team of two, taking turns patrolling and watching vigilantly from the observation tower. Their home base was several miles away, reachable only by air in winter. It was decades ago; primitive Russian surveillance equipment could never cut through. There were no unbreakable fences like today. The border was just an imaginary line, and two angry barracks stood facing each other on either side.

Below the flag poles through the gaps in the barrack walls, each side had artilleries placed that pointed toward each other. Heaps of grenades, semi-automatic weapons, and magazines took a giant portion of the living space in the barracks, leaving just enough room to crawl into the sleeping bag. Gunshots and shells flew over them each night like a ritual. When the real alert came from the base, they were ready in a few seconds. The real enemy was not the one everyone thought. Infiltrating terrorists from the training camps on the other side was ongoing in the cover of the darkness, making the region unstable. They were always prepared when they arrived, but the infiltrators took more risk in the wind that came with a bone-rattling chill and almost zero visibility. Most times Mother Nature failed them and the following day they would see many frozen bodies over the terrain.

The saying, 'keep your friends close, and your enemies closer' literally made sense in their case. Two enemy pickets waited and watched each other's moves constantly, building tension with every moment. During the day, they didn't even know if they should smile at each other and they exchanged unfriendly stares with the opposite side, continuing to do their surveillance and chores by taking turns. Intermittent songs caught by the transistor radio kept them entertained, something they look forward to in the late afternoons.

How long can you look at someone angrily? The mind is like the sky; sometimes it clears and brightens. Their attitude was changed by a little idea that sprung between them. It was on *Diwali,* a festival that symbolized the victory of good over evil. The food delivery crew dropped them an extra-large box of sweets. Alok, his partner, suggested giving this to the barracks on the other side, their enemy. He pointed out that Pakistani soldiers supported them with fires when infiltration of terrorists occurred. Terrorists were their common enemy. They both agreed on the idea of sharing the joy of *Diwali* with the other side, but the big question was how to deliver the box? The moment one crosses the border, the enemy fire could swallow him. Even in death, disgrace would follow for crossing the international border without following the proper procedures. After deliberate discussion, they decided to throw the packet to the other side. Then to gain attention, they fired into the sky, the same way the other side celebrated their holidays. They watched through the slits in the wall of the barracks. Three of them quickly went out with guns pointing and stood in position ready to attack. Uncle went out, gathering all his courage with his hands in the air, and wished them "Happy Diwali" and pointed toward the box of sweets.

From that day onwards nothing changed how they operated, but they were friends, friendship without borders. They used to share food, and play cards. The relief of not having to fear something that burdened the mind forever is indeed the greatest gift of one's freedom. As time passed, and the minds got lighter with fewer worries, they stayed focused on the common enemy. When there were tensions between the two countries, or one was getting the message from the base of danger, they used to shoot at the other bunker's direction without hurting anyone. On some nights when it was really quiet, they used to gather to play cards and sip from their rationed Old Monk Rum.

It was during one of those rivalries that Alex expressed his wild dream of going down the mountain to explore the countryside of Pakistan-owned Kashmir. He craved to get stoned by drinking *bhang*, which was a very popular drink made from cannabis in that region. Everyone laughed and thought he was crazy. Indeed, it was a crazy idea as it was unthinkable. It was true that when the brain has nothing to keep it busy, the blood will hesitate to flow and slows down to diminish the brain cells. It was obvious that the consequences of getting caught were beyond what anyone could think, but it didn't matter to him. He was certain it wouldn't be limited to undergoing court-martial, losing jobs, or getting jailed. In addition, it would invite huge disgrace to the family, and the 'betrayer' tab would follow for generations. But nothing worried him with rum in his belly; he was young and was mad about going to the enemy's den to get high.

After a few days, one of the Pak soldiers, Fayyaz, offered to take Uncle along with him when they went to collect rations and supplies. On the way, there was a place hidden in the mountains where he could have his wishes fulfilled, then come back when they returned. He joined the Pak soldier, disguising himself as a native traveler, carrying enough local money and his military outfit in the backpack.

Hiking down the steep mountainous area was so grueling; it took more than courage and skill. A slip or a wrong step on the narrow path could make one vanish into the steep ravines, where even the bones would disappear into dust. Journey in winter was impossible and a helicopter dropped supplies every other week. The risk was worth it for the lifetime experience of seeing the breathtaking view of the gorges and multi-layered glaciers on the faraway mountains. The shiny strip of the river looked like a silver necklace thrown onto the green. After an hour, they reached a place hidden from the world. It had a few wooden and stone houses that were stacked together like a honeycomb. The stone houses on the edge looked as if they were carved on the mountain with tiny passages between them. His friend, the Pakistani soldier, walked into a stone house with a wide wooden door.

Uncle had no idea what was waiting for him inside. As he entered, a seething air swept over him. Its pungent stench opened up every pore in his body, and his blood seemed to inhale it so much that he lost all his sensations. He feared suffocation for a moment and felt his nostrils to make sure he was still breathing. Slowly his blurry eyes cleared, and he began to see shadows moving among the smoke from the hundreds of hookahs lit like a thousand fireflies stuck to it.

With a soothing grin, Fayyaz said. "Don't worry, you will get used to it. It is a once-in-a-lifetime experience. Have no worries. No fears. I will go down and get supplies and grab you on my way back. Enjoy!"

He disappeared into the back room for a while and went on his way. After a few minutes of waiting, a boy around ten years old came with a clay pot filled with a dull green drink. He took a sip and another sip and another and soon it was all gone. Another full pot replaced the empty one. He noticed voices dragging but smiles brightened every face. For him, it was like watching a slow-moving movie where he sat idle in a corner of the screen, unnoticed. He snapped in and out of reality and slowly blended into the air and the smell bothered him no more.

First, he thought he was hallucinating. His hazy eyes zoomed in on a woman in a burka approaching him. She sat opposite him and asked, "Sir, would you like to smoke with some herbs, your friend told me to take care of you as well." She keenly watched him drink from the pot through the netted cover on her face.

"So, I guess you are not from here, right? No one drinks this way here."

For a moment, she lifted the cover over her face, giggled, and whispered, "Relax, India boy," and quickly walked away. He was stirred and ecstatic at the same time. His eyes followed her till she merged into clouds of smoke that whirled around on her path.

Did she reveal my identity aloud? Or was that just a fluke? Either way, she couldn't be harmful, he thought. Unsure he was, but her enigmatic face and ardent eyes made him curious and sparked an incomprehensible feeling within. He began to inhale the dazed vapor into his heart. Craning, he looked through the smoke circles he exhaled, hoping to see her again. Suddenly, it occurred to him that she didn't belong there, and he had a strong urge to know more about her. For a man in his early twenties, it was his instincts and the feeling that made him keep going; experiences and veracities were hindrances.

It was not just for a good time, but the urge to see her was driving Uncle Alex to keep visiting the joint. Some days she ignored him for no obvious reason, other days she would cling to him. Later that year, at the beginning of the *Ramadan* season, he went down the mountain. The door was closed and he knocked and waited patiently. There was no sign of anyone inside and he turned to go back, but his heart didn't. He knocked really hard, and then stuck his ear to the tiny slit on the wooden door. He listened for any movements inside. After a few minutes of waiting, he heard a feeble sound of footsteps approaching; he quickly recognized the movement.

She opened the door slowly to have a peek at the visitor who was at the door. When she saw him, she lifted the cover over her face and let him in. The place was empty, but he could hear people walking and murmurs were coming from inside the kitchen area.

"Do you know this place is closed this month till the sun sets?"

He shook his head while he seated himself on a worn-out divan. After fetching a pot of cold bhang, she sat opposite him and lit a hookah for him. She stared at him, her blazing eyes pierced into his and he felt a burn somewhere inside his chest. He was a bit embarrassed by the situation, but as a soldier trained to fight against the toughest enemies in brutal situations, he was able to gain his composure quickly and asked, "Is it real or the stench of the stale air from the past that is driving me crazy?"

"Do you come here because you like this place? Or anyway... you are not in love. Are you?" she asked him in a soft voice.

Stammering, he replied, "No... no, of course not. I haven't thought of such a thing." Saying that he quickly gulped what was left in the pot. She took the empty pot inside to get him another one. To overcome the uneasiness of the past episode, he took a few quick puffs from the hookah, rekindling the dying ember.

While bringing the refilled pot, she asked him, "Do you know who I am? You know nothing about the lives under this roof. This burqa is just a smooth cover; you really don't want to breathe what is burning inside."

There was silence for a few minutes. They avoided looking at each other, and then after a long pause, she began to tell her story. Her name was Saraswati, a Hindu girl from Kashmir. She was abducted one afternoon when she was walking home after school. She was taken to their hideout in the nearby forest where she was brutally tortured and beaten for several days. They hit her with a rod on her thighs, threatened to kill her family if she did not change her religion and marry one of the militant leaders. Uncle had sat speechless in disbelief. He was taking tiny sips from the pot to control his mounting angst.

"I am not the only one; it always happens to young women and teenage girls in Jammu and Kashmir. Many dreams are shattered at gunpoint, forcing us to save ourselves without any choice." There was a fire in her eyes when she said this.

She wanted to study and become a teacher, but her dreams were shattered after she was forcibly married to a militant. Ten months after her marriage, her childhood was snatched away when she delivered a son, but he died before he turned one.

"I didn't cry," she continued to speak from her heart. "You see those children working here... he would have been one of them, eventually forced to cross the border to carry out a ruthless mission. Maybe God loved him more than anyone else. He saved him before he blew himself up along with innocent people." She rubbed away her tears, but they kept dripping through her fingers. Uncle had closed his eyes for a moment to see a schoolgirl with kohl-lined eyes walking through the stone-paved road; her eventful life and her fate had brought her before him. *Why am I here listening to her? How can I give her hope?* He pondered.

Failure to find a way to console her made him feel tiny. Resentment brewed within him for his own helplessness. It turned into a feeling he couldn't control. He left in silence, hoping to come back, to give her reasons to be buoyant; he didn't promise anything as he didn't want her to fail again. His feelings toward her deepened and its warmth shielded him from the stinging cold air wanting to pierce through his spirit.

Uncle visited her whenever the weather was favorable and tension along the border was trivial. During winter afternoons, she snuck out with him to the valley as a couple might and hung out in Sufi shrines. They hid in its crowded basement where the rising intensity of *Qawwali* music made them disappear into a trance, wrapping them in the intoxicating fumes that pervaded its ambiance. Some days they exited the present, dancing with the spirits of the saints who took them to a rapturous state. Those were the best days of their lives which they hoped would last forever, but the aura of the saints' fire enveloping them didn't help to outlive their fate.

It was at the end of one of their outings when everything changed for good. When they returned it was night, the whole valley was under curfew. Like an unending thunder rolling, flairs and sounds from shelling and gunfire emerged all along the border. Helicopters were searching with floodlights, which lit every nook and corner of the region's darkness. It was rumored that hundreds of trained militants had infiltrated the Indian Territory. His entire body trembled, resonating with his drumming heartbeat, and he struggled hard to regain his composure. Neither the chilling northwest wind nor the relaxation techniques learned in the military academy could keep him cool. His precarious situation, brought on by himself, and the thought of the consequences of his inane actions, made him nervous. He weighed the graveness of living in the brutal Pakistani jail from where he might never see the sunshine for the rest of his life. And if he was spotted by the Indian helicopter in the Pakistan territory, he would be stamped as a betrayer for life, to live in disgrace.

Saraswati came close to him. After wiping the sweat off his forehead, she slowly ran her fingers through his ruffled hair and said, "Hey, brave soldier, you are born to fight fearlessly and to face even death with a smile. The storm will be over; you know what could be the worst thing that could happen to you. You could join me here; a long burqa will protect you when you are here." He stood up, looked at her, and slowly lifted her face cover and looked into her eyes. He whispered in her ear, "Don't you know, in this burqa, I will look much more beautiful than you?" They both burst into laughter and all his worries disappeared, at least for the moment.

He waited a few hours for everything to calm down, and for the border to come to some kind of normalcy. Then he cut through the bushes and fog to the place where his uniform and gun were hidden. He changed into the military outfit and hiked toward the border that was almost a mile away from the picket. The nourishing cold wind gave him the strength to be himself and he felt he had already won the greatest war and was ready to take on another one.

When he reached the border, he looked up at the dull, gray sky and took a deep breath. Then he closed his eyes and jumped into the trench that was dug very deep to keep the enemies from crossing. Everything else was just a distant memory from there. When he opened his eyes, he was in the military hospital, covered in a body cast. He had several broken bones and had a severe back injury. It took almost six months for his treatment and rehabilitation before he went back to duty.

Uncle then pointed toward a medal that was hung on the wall and said, "Can you believe it? That was the Medal of Honor I received for that night. My colleague covered me. He said I volunteered to go check out some suspicious movement on the border and didn't see me after that. Even the helicopters couldn't find me until the next morning. My pictures were in the newspaper."

Ashok couldn't wait to hear the closure of the story and asked, "Did you meet her again?"

Dissolving into silent laughter, Uncle replied, "After recovering, they felt I wouldn't be fit enough for combat jobs. I was posted in New Delhi at a desk job. I really wanted to go back and cross the border to see her again. But our wishes rarely align with fate. See... now I am here on the other side of the world sipping Old Monk with you, recreating my memories to live in."

Ashok didn't know what to say, but he recited verses from the Indian epic Mahabharata where Lord Krishna advised the confused *Pandava* prince *Arjuna* over the battle of *Kurukshetra.*

"Whatever happened, happened for the good; Whatever is happening, is happening for the good; Whatever will happen, will also happen for the good only. You need not have any regrets about the past. You need not worry about the future. The present is happening ..."

By the time Ashok and Nila headed home, it was dark and they didn't speak to each other. Nila was worried. Ashok would scold her for leaving him alone to the garrulous uncle to die of boredom. But Ashok was in the hangover period of the most breathtaking stories he had heard from an uncle, which Nila had no clue about. During this trip, Ashok realized his outlook on life and people had changed quite a bit. Uncle Alex, a simple man whom he believed to be just a loquacious bragger, helped him redefine his views. He always felt that he had nothing to contribute and he took ordinary lives for granted. He realized everyone was different with unique experiences and had a role to play in this big world. While on the highway, they had old, nostalgic Hindi songs playing in the background. While passing through a *deer crossing* warning sign, Ashok remembered Uncle's hunting story. He would slow down for every road-kill on the way to see if there was someone in tears waiting nearby.

The End